JADA JONES

★ SKY WATCHER ★

JADA JONES

★ SKY WATCHER ★

by Kelly Starling Lyons
illustrated by Nneka Myers

Penguin Workshop

PENGUIN WORKSHOP
An Imprint of Penguin Random House LLC, New York

Text copyright © 2021 by Kelly Starling Lyons. Cover illustration copyright
© 2021 by Vanessa Brantley Newton. Illustrations copyright © 2021 by
Penguin Random House LLC. All rights reserved. Published by Penguin Workshop,
an imprint of Penguin Random House LLC, New York. PENGUIN and
PENGUIN WORKSHOP are trademarks of Penguin Books Ltd, and the W colophon
is a registered trademark of Penguin Random House LLC.
Manufactured in China.

Visit us online at www.penguinrandomhouse.com.

Library of Congress Cataloging-in-Publication Data is available upon request.

ISBN 9780593226469 (paperback)   10 9 8 7 6 5 4 3 2 1 LP
ISBN 9780593226476 (library binding)   10 9 8 7 6 5 4 3 2 1 LP

For my children and kids
everywhere, there's no ceiling on
your dreams. Look up and fly—KSL

For all my family and friends
who encourage me to reach for
the stars and beyond—NM

Chapter One: STAR LIGHT, STAR BRIGHT

Once the stars started to shimmer in the ebony sky, we headed outside. Mom set up the telescope in our backyard. We huddled around it, waiting for our chance to gaze into the dark blanket of night.

My little brother, Jackson, went first. He squeezed one eye shut and pressed the other against the glass.

"It's not working right," he said, like he was ready to give up.

"It takes practice," Mom replied. "You can do it. Keep going."

Mom said when she was little like Jax, she tried to use her dad's telescope over and over. Then, one day, the lessons he gave her clicked. She could see planets, constellations, nebulas. Baby steps: That's what she always says gets you to a goal. One foot in front of the other.

"Here, Jax," I said, giving him binoculars. "Remember how to use these?"

"Wow," he responded. "Everything looks so close!"

"You're up, Jada," Dad said.

I peered through the lens at sparkling diamonds of light and thought about my hero Dr. Mae C. Jemison, the first Black woman astronaut. How did she feel flying on a space shuttle? What did Earth look like from way up there? Was she nervous to be so far from home, or thrilled by the adventure? I think I'd be a mix of both—full of excitement at exploring, and maybe missing my family, too. I'd love to ask her what it was like one day.

"Spot anything cool?" Dad asked.

I got a chill when I saw what

looked like a lemonade-colored
star. It didn't twinkle and had rings
around it. I gasped. Was that what I
thought it was?

"Mom! I think I see Saturn."

Mom took a peek.

"Exactly right," she said, smiling.

"Can I see it again?" I stared and stared and never wanted it to end. Mom calls me a sky-watcher-in-training. She's teaching me to see the wonders of space.

After everyone got a turn, it was time for bed. I headed upstairs and pulled out my Dream Big journal, where I keep a list of my goals. Near the top were "go to space camp" and "visit the Grand Canyon." I pulled out my four-in-one pen, clicked to purple, and added a new goal: "meet Mae Jemison."

I looked at my poster of her in a

space suit, head held high. I smiled, made a wish, turned off the light, and snuggled in my daybed. Glow-in-the-dark stars on the ceiling turned my room into a galaxy. I drifted to sleep imagining I was on a rocket to the sky.

At school, my teacher, Miss Taylor, introduced a new project.

"Has anyone ever been to a wax museum that's filled with statues of famous people?"

A couple of hands shot up.

"What if the statues could talk?"

"Now *that's* the museum for me," said my friend Simone.

We laughed. Each morning, Simone appears on our classroom TV screen for *BE News*, the morning announcement show for our school, Brookside Elementary. I could just see her interviewing the statues and getting the scoop. She knew how to work it.

"We're going to create a living museum," Miss Taylor said. "Each of you will pick someone who has made a difference, do research on their life, and make a display. In a couple weeks, you'll pretend you're statues that have come to life and talk about the important things you've done. Your families can even attend."

The beads on my braids sung as I bounced in my seat. I already knew who I wanted to be. I'd hoped to play Mae Jemison in last year's Black History Month play, but I froze at the audition. I could see the lines in my mind, but it was like someone zipped my lips shut. Nothing came out but a squeak. Now, I was getting a do-over. I pictured Mae Jemison smiling on my poster. This was my chance to make her proud.

I turned to my buddy Lena, who sat beside me.

"Who are you going to be?"

"A writer," she replied. That's

what I thought she'd say. Lena had notebooks filled with fantastic stories. She even had one published in a magazine for kids.

"Okay, let's line up to go to the media center," Miss Taylor said. "Time to find some inspiration."

"I need someone fierce," Simone said, striking a pose. Her shirt had a sequined star that shined like she was on stage. "Bold and brilliant like me."

We laughed and headed down the hallway. The media specialist, Mr. Agyeman, had stacks of books ready. We zipped over like bees zooming to a field of flowers. The room buzzed as everyone looked for their perfect fit for the project.

"Whoa, slow down, friends," he said. "I appreciate your enthusiasm. But don't worry. The books aren't going anywhere."

My heart skipped when I saw the picture book *Mae Among the Stars.* I found a cozy spot and read about Mae Jemison as a little girl, dreaming of seeing Earth from space. She worked hard as she grew up and achieved her goal.

"Any more about Mae Jemison?" I asked Mr. Agyeman.

"Do I have more?" he said, gesturing to the packed shelves all around. "Ask and you shall receive."

He pointed out books filled with biographies of famous people. In one, I learned that Dr. Jemison's favorite subject was science, like mine. She enjoyed trying her older brother's and sister's experiments. In another, I found out that she started college at sixteen and learned to speak several languages.

But then a funny thing happened. The more I read about how incredible Dr. Jemison was, the more I got a sinking feeling. She was amazing.

Maybe *too* amazing. Did I have what it took to bring her to life?

"Check it out," Miles said, showing me his book, *Ticktock Banneker's Clock*. I saw that he was saying something else, but all I could hear were my thoughts. What if I wasn't the best person to play Mae Jemison? What if I didn't measure up?

"Jada, isn't that cool?" Miles asked.

"Huh?" I said as I tuned back in. "Sorry. What did you say?"

"Benjamin Banneker made the first clock in America. He taught himself how to do it and carved it out of wood."

"Awesome."

At the end of our media center visit, Mr. Agyeman asked us to share our picks.

"I want to be Stan Lee," Carson said. "He's the man. He created superheroes like the Hulk."

"I picked Laurie Hernandez," Gabi said. "She won gold with Team USA at the Olympics and silver on the balance beam."

I raised my hand.

"Dr. Mae Jemison?" I planned to say it loud and proud, but it came out like a question.

"You sure, Jada?" Mr. Agyeman asked.

I nodded.

"Let's hear it again. With

confidence this time."

"I will be Mae Jemison, the first Black woman in space."

I said it like I meant it. Now, I just had to make it come true.

Chapter Two:
TRAILBLAZERS

I decided to learn everything I could about Mae Jemison. I had to get it just right. I read articles about her online, and watched videos of her talking. She said that a character on *Star Trek* inspired her. Seeing Lieutenant Nyota Uhura, a Black woman, flying on a spaceship made her dream of doing it, too. I smiled wide and raced downstairs. I knew someone who loves that show.

"Mom, did you know that Mae Jemison watched *Star Trek* just like you?"

"I'm not surprised," she said. "I used to watch reruns of the original series with my dad. You can't help but imagine yourself in space, too."

I tried to picture Mom as an astronaut wearing an orange NASA suit and boots. It was fun imagining her shooting through the stars.

"What made you want to be a librarian?" I asked.

"I decided to help kids explore new worlds through books. Did you know that actress Nichelle Nichols almost left *Star Trek*? Dr. Martin

Luther King Jr. convinced her to stay."

"Dr. King? He was a fan?"

"Yes ma'am," she said. "She continued in her role in the series and in movies, going up in rank from lieutenant to commander. What she did was bigger than play a part on a TV show. She helped kids around the nation dream big dreams, just like how Dr. Jemison is inspiring you. One day, you'll inspire kids, too."

I got a queasy feeling in my stomach. I didn't know about that. Nichelle Nichols and Mae Jemison were trailblazers. I wasn't even sure I could do a good job on my project.

"Did somebody say *Star Wars*?" Jax said, running into the room with his

lightsaber drawn. It glowed purple
and hummed as he sliced the air.

"No, Jax, we were talking about *Star Trek*."

"Jedis rule," he said and dashed away.

I went to my room and looked over my notes. Mae Jemison did so much. She was a doctor, engineer, astronaut. Where should I start? I sighed and leaned my cheek against my fist.

Dad knocked on my open door and came in with a big grin. How did he always know when I needed a boost?

"Guess who's speaking at Duke University?"

I shrugged.

"That's no fun," he said. "Here's a

clue. She was on the space shuttle *Endeavour* and her number one fan lives in our house."

I jumped up and squealed.

"No way!"

I felt like I was floating with stars swirling around me. I couldn't believe it.

"Mae Jemison!"

"You got it. The tickets are free. I'll try to get some as soon as reservations open."

I rushed over and hugged him. Then, the project popped back into my mind. I really needed to nail it, now that I might actually have the chance to meet her. How could I look her in the eye if I messed up?

Chapter Three:
MOON MANIA

In science, we were studying space. Miss Taylor always makes lessons fun. That day, she had paper plates, napkins, and Popsicle sticks set out on each table. There were also charts of the phases of the moon.

"Okay, everyone," she said when we got settled into our seats. "I'm going to pass out cookies. No eating."

We groaned.

"Yet," she said with a wink.

"What do you think we're doing?" Lena whispered.

I shrugged, but my mind started racing. When I saw that they were chocolate sandwich cookies, I sat up straight.

"Anyone figure out what the cookies are for?" Miss Taylor asked.

Both my hand and Miles's shot up.

"Jada."

"We're going to use them to show each phase of the moon."

"Exactly right."

I could already see how it would work. A whole cookie would be the new moon—that's when it looks totally or almost completely dark. A cookie with the top off and just the cream showing would be a full moon. We could use the popsicle stick to reveal slivers of cream or cookie to create the other ones.

Our table split up the work. We each got to create a couple of phases. I worked on a crescent moon, but the cookie kept breaking.

"Need help, Jada?" Carson asked.

I shook my head and kept working.

"Are you sure, Jada?" Lena asked, eyeing the broken tries on the table.

"I got it," I said with more bite than I meant. "Sorry, Lena. I can do it."

I took a breath and finally got it. Miss Taylor walked around, nodding as she looked at our creations.

"Good job, everyone," she said. "For your reward, you can eat the cookies you worked on."

"Science is delicious," Simone said as she gobbled her cookies.

"Let's see what you've learned," Miss Taylor said.

"I knew there was a catch," RJ said.

Even Miss Taylor laughed at that.

"We're just going over what we've been studying," she replied. "Your quiz is Monday. Okay, here we go: What creates the light of the moon?"

Miles beat me to the answer.

"The reflection of the sun."

"What's a gibbous moon?"

Miles had his hand up again. We're always the top two in science. Usually, it's a friendly competition. But this time, him getting the answer before me felt like a tiny splinter that's stuck in your finger. It's not big enough to really hurt, but it bothers you enough to notice. I sighed and thought about Mae Jemison. I had to try harder.

The next time Miss Taylor asked a question, my hand was up before she even finished.

"Jada."

Uh-oh. What did she say? Did she want to know about the moon appearing to get larger or smaller? I crossed my fingers and guessed.

"When it looks smaller, it's called waning," I said.

"That's right," she said. "But I was asking about it looking larger. Remember to wait until I give the whole question."

I hung my head. It felt bad when Miles was beating me to every answer. Felt worse that I got it wrong and was corrected in front of everyone.

"Lena."

"The moon is waxing when it looks larger."

"Good job," I heard Miss Taylor say.

She dimmed the lights and showed us some pictures from the moon. One was a shot of footprints. Since there's no atmosphere there, they can last for decades. People in history make big marks. Could I fill Mae Jemison's boots?

I couldn't wait for lunch so I could focus on something else.

Simone, Lena, and I settled at the table with our trays.

"Want to come over after school?" I asked between bites of mac and cheese. Friday was the official start to weekend fun.

"Sorry, can't make it today," Simone said. "I'm going shopping to get some supplies for my project. I'm loving being Oprah Winfrey. Do you know people called her the Queen of Talk? Perfect for me, or what?"

"I'm having fun with mine, too," Lena said. "I'm going to perform one of Nikki Giovanni's poems. Maybe we can get together this weekend."

"Sure," I said, trying to hide my disappointment at not being able to hang out with my BFFs that day. "That would be cool."

"How's your project going, Jada?" Simone asked. "Bet you got it all figured out."

I tried to smile, but inside I groaned. If they only knew how far that was from the truth. I had notes, but no idea of where to begin. I hadn't even started putting together my display. I thought I'd made a mistake. Dr. Jemison was my hero, but it seemed like she always had everything together. How could I convince people I was her when I felt like I was falling apart?

Everyone else was having fun. I heard RJ telling Miles that he was bringing in some old-school video game cartridges to show the tech his trailblazer invented. Maybe I should switch to someone else while I had time.

That was it! A smile stretched across my face. Why hadn't I thought of that before? I could ask Miss Taylor if I could change to someone else, someone I could be without a sweat. That could be my answer.

I felt like dancing as we headed out for recess. We went right to the ropes.

"Jada, can you turn with Lena?" Simone asked. "I want to practice my moves."

Simone did donkey kicks. Lena went next and did a cartwheel into the ropes. When I was up, I watched the rhythm for the right time to run inside. As the ropes whirred around

me, I got in the zone where you feel
like you can keep going forever.
But as my feet tapped out a beat,
I felt guilt nagging me again. Mae
Jemison would never give up. Maybe
I shouldn't either.

It wasn't that long ago that I
didn't know how to jump double
Dutch. Lena and Simone taught me
a little at a time. I took a breath and
ran out of the ropes perfectly. Baby
steps—that's what Mom always says.
I'd give the project one more try. I
owed Dr. Jemison that. If it didn't
work out, I'd tell Miss Taylor on
Monday that I needed to switch.

Chapter Four:
JOURNEY INTO SPACE

Mom had a surprise for me when I got home.

"Since you're going to be the first Black woman astronaut for the wax museum, I thought we could go to Morehead Planetarium."

Usually I'd be all in. That's one of my favorite places, but I wasn't sure if I'd stick with being Mae Jemison. I shifted my feet.

"I was actually thinking that I might change to someone else," I said slowly and cautiously. "I'm going to decide by Monday."

Mom could read me like one of her books at story time.

"Really?" she said. "I'm surprised. I thought you were excited about being Mae Jemison. Well, we can still go. Always cool to see the stars."

Whew. Mom had let me off easy. Jax and Dad were running errands, so it was just us. I hopped in Ruby— what Mom called her maroon Jeep— and we headed to Chapel Hill. We bopped to Beyoncé as we got on I-40. Then, Mom turned down the music. Uh-oh. I knew what that meant.

"So tell me what's up," she said. "Why don't you want to be Mae Jemison?"

I thought about saying I found someone I wanted to be more, but that wasn't true. I sighed and fessed up.

"I'm trying, but I just can't get it together," I said. "She was fearless, great in everything. I feel like a flop. I can't figure out what I want to say in my speech. Science isn't fun anymore."

"Take it easy on yourself," she said. "Remember you're pretty amazing, too. I bet Mae Jemison didn't have it together every day. None of us do."

I listened to the music, but my head was filled with Mom's words. I'd been focusing on all of the great things Mae Jemison did. I wondered if she had struggles just like I did.

When we got to Morehead, we sat in the planetarium. All around us the Carolina sky came to life. It swept me away. I wasn't sitting in my seat anymore—I was on a rocket zooming through stars. A chill ran up my arms like when I saw Saturn through the telescope. With the room a velvet night, constellations lit up the dome. I was in another world.

On the way out, we stopped by the gift shop. I saw astronaut ice cream, rocket kits, and star maps and got that chill again. I knew I couldn't change my hero. I had to figure this out.

At home, Dad called me to the living room. He frowned like something was wrong.

"I'm sorry, Jada," he said. "I forgot about the Mae Jemison tickets."

Oh no. I stared at the floor. Thinking about seeing her made my heart race with nerves, but deep inside I'd hoped it would happen.

"That's okay," I said, looking up again.

"Is it?" he asked, holding out his phone. " Because I remembered and just got them online.

But if you don't want them, I can give them away."

"Daaaad!"

He got me. I hugged him tight and walked away with a grin that shone like the sun. My wish was coming true.

I went to my desk on a mission: Time to do more research. Instead of just focusing on Mae Jemison's achievements, I looked for the hurdles. What kind of challenges did she face? What did she overcome? Mom was right. Everybody has something they're dealing with.

As I scanned through articles, one line made my eyes pop and my mouth hang open. Had I really read what I thought I had? I looked at it again. There it was in bold, black letters: "As a kid, Mae Jemison was scared of heights." How was that possible? She wanted to be an astronaut when she was little! I'd never thought of her being afraid of anything. Maybe we had more in common than I'd thought.

Chapter Five:
MAKING IT RIGHT

I was walking up the steps to the fourth grade hallway before I realized I'd been so busy focusing on my Mae Jemison project that I forgot to study. The moon quiz was today.

I entered the room with a feeling of dread and sank into my seat.

"What's wrong, Jada?" Lena asked when she saw my long face.

"I'm okay. Wish I had more time to get ready."

As Miss Taylor passed out the papers face down, I closed my eyes, trying to remember the answers on the study sheet.

"Okay, everybody can turn their quiz over and start," Miss Taylor said.

When I saw what was there, I knew I was in trouble. Vocabulary words. Phases of the moon. I thought I knew the answers, but I wasn't sure. I wrote something down and erased it. Then, I wrote down something else and wasn't sure if that was right, either. I saw Miles finish first and turn his paper over. Then, others did the same. I sighed and tried my best.

"How'd you do, Jada?" Miles asked, sitting next to me on the orange and blue carpet for our next lesson.

"Not great," I said.

I didn't really feel like talking. I scooted over a little and looked away. Miles didn't say anything else. When I looked back, I saw that he was sitting next to RJ.

Every time Miles answered a question, it was like that little splinter was back. I couldn't see it, but it was there. Bothering me. I didn't know why I was letting Miles's shine get me down. It never had before. We were both in science club and on student council. We rooted for each other. Well, we used to. Now I felt like he was zooming to the finish line while I was jogging backward.

Miss Taylor assigned us into groups. I was with Miles, Simone, and

Carson. We talked about why day and night happen and then worked on our diagrams. We each had to create a picture of our own.

"Miles, that looks great," Carson said, gazing at his drawing of Earth.

After a while, everyone in the group was done but me. I kept working, trying to add more details. If I made this really good, maybe it would help make up for the quiz if I hadn't done so well on it.

"Nice," Miles said. "When you're done, we can compare what we drew."

The splinter was back. This time, I couldn't ignore it. Before I knew it, I was blurting something I regretted.

"Sorry not everyone is as fast as you."

"Dang, Jada," Simone said.

I sneaked a look at Miles.

His eyebrows were scrunched, and his lips were tight. Why had I said that? He was a good friend. I'd messed up, and I knew I had to make it right. I waited until we were lining up for lunch.

"Miles, do you want to come over to my house one day and work on our museum projects together?"

"Why would you want me over?" he asked. "I thought I was a show-off."

I didn't blame him for being annoyed. I tried to talk to him at lunch, but he was always in the middle of talking to someone else. My next chance was at recess as he waited for his turn at kickball.

He saw me walking over and turned the other way. I deserved that. My stomach twisted, but I took a breath and went up to him. I'd gotten myself into this; I had to try to fix it.

"I'm sorry," I said, standing next to him as we watched Gabi run the bases. "I was really mad at myself. I didn't mean to take it out on you."

"That wasn't cool," he said. "But I

get it. I bug out sometimes, too."

"Bug out? I didn't say I was bugging."

Miles tilted his head and gave me a look like we both knew how I was acting.

"Okay, maybe a little."

We laughed.

"I meant it about inviting you over. Want to come?"

"Sure," he said.

"Great! I'll ask my mom to call yours."

Later, while we were working on our projects, I found out that his hero, Benjamin Banneker, was also an astronomer. He even made an almanac and predicted a solar eclipse.

"I read that he loved to watch the stars," Miles said.

"Really? Mae Jemison did too. That's how she started dreaming of being an astronaut."

I showed Miles our telescope and told him about seeing Saturn for the first time. He liked space, too. His uncle lives in Florida, and he took him to Kennedy Space Center to see a rocket launch.

I told him about discovering some of Mae Jemison's fears.

"Wow," Miles said. "I never thought about astronauts being afraid of things when they were little. They're just like us."

I leaned forward. When Miles said that, it was like a light turned on in my head. I scribbled my idea into my notebook, nodding.

It was different from what I was going for, but felt good. Mae Jemison never did just what was expected. She blazed her own path. I was celebrating her my way—this could work.

WAX MUSEUM

Chapter Six:
SHOWTIME

The next week, we set up for the wax museum in the cafeteria. Everybody had a table to show off their hero. Miles had on overalls and studied a pocket watch. Lena was wearing her curly 'fro loose and had a display board of poems. Simone rocked a colorful dress and held a microphone. I looked around. I was the only one dressed like a kid.

I had on my blue NASA T-shirt and orange cargo pants. On my table, I'd placed a telescope made out of paper towel rolls and a helmet made out of a cardboard box, like the illustration in *Mae Among the Stars*. I had a picture I'd drawn of Lieutenant Uhura from *Star Trek* and what Earth looks like from space.

As parents walked through the exhibits, I practiced in my head and tried to stop fidgeting. I could do this. I had memorized my lines and had index cards, too, just in case. When someone came to my table, I was ready.

"My name is Mae Carol Jemison," I said. "Sometimes I'm scared of heights. But what I'm more afraid of is not following my dreams. One day, I'm going to fly to the stars."

As I shared Mae Jemison's dreams and what she grew up to achieve, my shakiness faded away. If she could face her fears, I could too. Dr. Jemison and I could do anything.

I saw Mom and Dad coming

and felt my heart race. I hadn't let them hear my speech in advance because I wanted it to be a surprise. Mr. Agyeman walked up and joined them. I remembered him telling me to be confident, so I gave it my all.

They clapped when I finished.

"No question," Mr. Agyeman said. "You brought Dr. Jemison to life. Well done."

Dad hugged my shoulder.

"We're so proud of you," Mom said.

After the parents left, we got to walk around and check out everyone else's exhibits. Kids raised their hands for the chance to be interviewed by Oprah played by

Simone. Lena recited one of Nikki Giovanni's poems and one of her own. Miles talked about his hero carving the first clock with wood from his farm. Kids were loving Carson's comics and Gabi's medals.

Then it was time for them to visit my table. My friends looked through my paper-towel-roll telescope and tried on the box helmet.

"Jada, you were all quiet about your project," Simone said. "Knew you had something good."

She would never believe what really went on.

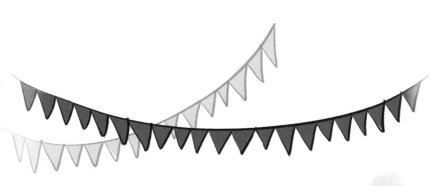

At home that evening, Mom set up the telescope.

"I think in celebration of Jada's starring role as Dr. Mae Jemison, it's time for some stargazing."

Jax was up first. He looked through the eyepiece and was completely quiet. Then he broke into a smile and began to jump in place.

"I can see a crater on the moon!"

I remembered how it felt the first time I saw something special—I was hooked. When it was my turn to gaze through the telescope, I looked into the sky and didn't just see the

moon. I pictured myself going to space one day.

In my room, I was too excited to sleep. I smiled at my Mae Jemison poster. Then, I turned off the lights, hopped on my bed, and stared at my ceiling canopy of stars. Just one more day until I saw her. It couldn't come fast enough!

Chapter Seven:
BEING ME

It was cool being out on a school night. Duke University was huge! As we walked to Page Auditorium, I was glad Dad had said he and Jax would sit this one out so Mom and I could have some quality time. It meant a lot to share this with her. I used to just think of Dr. Jemison as a hero. But now, with everything I'd learned, she felt like a friend, too.

We sat as close to the front as we could and waited for Dr. Jemison to step on stage.

I looked at people filling the seats around us. They were different ages and races, there to see the first Black woman astronaut. They chattered with excitement as the big moment neared.

I held my head high in my NASA T-shirt and saw a couple of kids wearing orange space suits.

I wondered if they were sky watchers like me. What did they imagine when they gazed at the stars? What wonders had they seen?

When Dr. Jemison arrived, she was a magnet drawing everyone's eyes to her. The room went quiet like someone had turned off the volume. She talked about being a kid who looked up and asked herself if others were seeing what she saw. She wanted astronauts to travel beyond our solar system in the next hundred years. When she said we're all connected with the universe, goose bumps covered my arms.

"What did you think?" Mom asked.

My heart dropped when Dr. Jemison got ready to leave for a reception. I rushed to the front and handed someone from Duke my picture of Lieutenant Uhura to give her—I hoped she liked it. I remembered a quote of hers I'd read in a magazine article: "The thing that I have done throughout my life is to do the best job that I can and to be me."

I stood up tall. Dr. Jemison was confident in being herself. I was too. Anything was possible one step at a time.

Just then, my eyes met Dr. Jemison's. I smiled and she grinned back. My feet were no longer on the ground. It felt like I was soaring

ACKNOWLEDGMENTS

I'm so excited to continue Jada's adventures. Thank you to everyone who has read and recommended the books, and added them to home, school, and library collections. This series is a tribute to all of the brilliant kids around the world who stand out and shine just by being who they are.

Special shout-out to Astronaut StarBright. A teen with big dreams and a big heart, Taylor Richardson of Jacksonville, Florida, is a student space ambassador and STEM advocate. Taylor has won national honors for being a changemaker. Among her contributions are raising thousands of dollars to send girls to see *Hidden Figures* and *A Wrinkle in Time* and donating more than ten thousand books to kids worldwide. Taylor plans to be an astronaut who travels to Mars. One of her heroes is Dr. Mae C. Jemison, just like Jada.

Thank you to Colleen Scott, director of the Baldwin Scholars program at Duke University. She organized Dr. Jemison's visit to Page Auditorium and gave me invaluable insights for this story.

As always, thank you to my editor Renee, agent Caryn, illustrators Nneka and Vanessa, and the entire Penguin Workshop team. This book wouldn't be possible without them and the circle of support that surrounds me—my family, friends, sorors, and each of you.

And now, here's a
sneak peek at the next

JADA JONES

★ NATURE LOVER ★

"Whoa. What's the rush, Jada?" Daddy asked.

I looked down and couldn't believe I'd already gobbled my two supersize banana pancakes.

"They were delicious," I said as I hurried to the sink. I blasted water on my flowered plate and stuck it in the dishwasher. My plate and silverware clattered as I slammed the door shut.

"Careful, Jada," Mom said. "I know you're excited, but you have time. Pop Pop won't arrive for another twenty minutes."

"Sorry," I said, and zipped upstairs to grab the purple backpack I stocked last night.

Water, snacks, journal, and my four-in-one pen for notes. I was all set. Field trip day with Pop Pop! I didn't want to miss a minute.

I raced down the stairs, stuck my paper bag lunch in my backpack, and stood by the door. I couldn't believe Pop Pop was going to be one of our chaperones on the nature trail. I'd finally get to show him off to my friends—and show him what I knew about plants and bugs.

"You get to have all the fun," my little brother, Jackson, said, scrunching his eyebrows as he stood beside me. "Why do you get to take Pop Pop on a field trip and I don't?"

"Bet he'll chaperone your next one," I said. "Just ask him."

I peeked out the window and squealed when I saw Betsy Brown Sugar, Pop Pop's station wagon, pulling up. Right on time.